Christmas is Coming

A Random House PICTUREBACK®

Library of Congress Cataloging-in-Publication Data:
Morehead, Ruth J. Christmas is coming, with Ruth J. Morehead's Holly Babes. p. cm.—(A Random House pictureback) SUMMARY: Presents texts for well-known Christmas songs and carols ISBN: 0-679-80075-1 (pbk.) 1. Christmas music—Texts. [1. Christmas music] I. Title.
PZ8.3.M797Ch 1989 783.6′5—dc19 89-3717

Manufactured in the United States of America 7 8 9 10

Christmas is Coming

With Ruth J. Morehead's Holly Babes™

A Book of Poems and Songs

Random House New York

We Three Kings of Orient Are

We three kings of Orient are;
Bearing gifts, we travel afar,
Field and fountain, moor and mountain,
Following yonder star.

O star of wonder, star of night,
Star with royal beauty bright,
Westward leading, still proceeding,
Guide us to thy perfect light.

John Henry Hopkins

A Christmas Card for Santa

We all hung up our stockings,
and we left you a nice snack.
By now, I guess, dear Santa,
you have filled your heavy pack.

Be careful, please, dear Santa,
on the rooftops where you go.
They're slanty and they're slippery
with a crust of ice and snow.

I guess I should be tired,
but I cannot fall asleep.
Tonight I'll count some reindeer
instead of counting sheep.

I think you are the nicest man
to do the things you do.
Merry Christmas, Santa dear,
and a happy New Year, too!

Bobbi Katz

Christmas Cookies

Clitter, clatter
baking tins,
cookie cutters,
rolling pin.
Christmas cookies. Let's begin!

Sugar, flour, eggs, and butter—
mixing bowls, a wooden spoon.

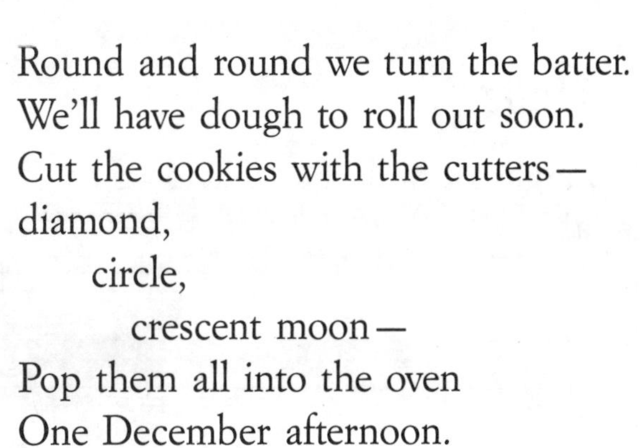

Round and round we turn the batter.
We'll have dough to roll out soon.
Cut the cookies with the cutters—
diamond,
    circle,
        crescent moon—
Pop them all into the oven
One December afternoon.

Bobbi Katz

Deck the Halls

Deck the halls with boughs of holly,
Fa la la la la la la la la!
'Tis the season to be jolly,
Fa la la la la la la la la!
Don we now our gay apparel,
Fa la la la la la la la la!
Troll the ancient yuletide carol,
Fa la la la la la la la la!

See the blazing yule before us,
Fa la la la la la la la la!
Strike the harp and join the chorus,
Fa la la la la la la la la!
Follow me in merry measure,
Fa la la la la la la la la!
While I tell of yuletide treasure,
Fa la la la la la la la la!

Silent Night

Silent night, holy night,
All is calm, all is bright.
Round yon Virgin mother and child,
Holy infant so tender and mild,
Sleep in heavenly peace,
Sleep in heavenly peace.

Joseph Mohr

Away in a Manger

Away in a manger,
No crib for a bed,
The little Lord Jesus
Laid down his sweet head.
The stars in the sky
Looked down where he lay,
The little Lord Jesus
Asleep on the hay.

Jingle Bells

Jingle bells, jingle bells,
Jingle all the way!
Oh what fun it is to ride
In a one-horse open sleigh!

Dashing through the snow,
In a one-horse open sleigh,
Over the fields we go,
Laughing all the way.

Jingle bells, jingle bells,
Jingle all the way!
Oh what fun it is to ride
In a one-horse open sleigh!

Bells on bobtail ring,
Making spirits bright;
What fun it is to ride
And sing a sleighing song tonight!

James Pierpont

O Christmas Tree

O Christmas tree, O Christmas tree,
Thy leaves are so unchanging.
O Christmas tree, O Christmas tree,
Thy leaves are so unchanging.
Not only green when summer's here,
But also when 'tis cold and drear.
O Christmas tree, O Christmas tree,
Thy leaves are so unchanging.

O Christmas tree, O Christmas tree,
You fill all hearts with gaiety.
O Christmas tree, O Christmas tree,
You fill all hearts with gaiety.
On Christmas Day you stand so tall,
Affording joy to one and all.
O Christmas tree, O Christmas tree,
You fill all hearts with gaiety.

Joy to the World

Joy to the world!
the Lord is come;
Let earth receive her king.
Let every heart
prepare him room,
and heaven and nature sing,
and heaven and nature sing,
And heaven, and heaven
and nature sing.

Isaac Watts

Hark! The Herald Angels Sing

Hark! the herald angels sing,
Glory to the newborn king!
Peace on earth and mercy mild,
God and sinners reconciled.
Joyful, all ye nations, rise,
Join the triumph of the skies;
With angelic host proclaim,
Christ is born in Bethlehem!
Hark! the herald angels sing,
Glory to the newborn king!

Charles Wesley

What Can I Give Him?

What can I give Him,
Poor as I am?
If I were a shepherd
I would bring a lamb,
If I were a Wise Man
I would do my part,
Yet what can I give Him,
Give my heart.

Christina Rossetti

O Little Town of Bethlehem

O little town of Bethlehem,
How still we see thee lie!
Above thy deep and dreamless sleep,
The silent stars go by.
Yet in thy dark streets shineth
The everlasting light;
The hopes and fears of all the years
Are met in thee tonight.

Phillips Brooks

I Saw Three Ships

I saw three ships come sailing in,
On Christmas Day, on Christmas Day;
I saw three ships come sailing in,
On Christmas Day in the morning.

And what was in those ships all three?
On Christmas Day, on Christmas Day;
And what was in those ships all three?
On Christmas Day in the morning.

Our Savior Christ and his lady
On Christmas Day, on Christmas Day;
Our Savior Christ and his lady
On Christmas Day in the morning.

Jack Frost

Someone painted pictures on my
Windowpane last night—
Willow trees with trailing boughs
And flowers—frosty white
And lovely crystal butterflies;
But when the morning sun
Touched them with its golden beams,
They vanished one by one!

Helen Bayley Davis

We Wish You a Merry Christmas

We wish you a merry Christmas,
We wish you a merry Christmas,
We wish you a merry Christmas and a happy New Year.
Good tidings to you, wherever you are,
Good tidings for Christmas and a happy New Year.

Good tidings we bring to you and your kin,
Good tidings for Christmas and a happy New Year.

Decorations

We are making decorations
To hang up on our tree.
We are cutting,
snipping,
pasting,
We're as busy as can be.
Bells and snowflakes,
Jolly Santas,
For the top a silver star
Like the shiny star the Three Kings saw
And followed from afar!

Bobbi Katz

Do Not Open Until Christmas

I shake-shake,
Shake-shake,
Shake the package well.

But what there is
Inside of it,
Shaking will not tell.

James S. Tippett

The Animals' Christmas

Jesus, our brother, kind and good,
Was humbly born in a stable rude;
And the friendly beasts around him stood,
Jesus, our brother, kind and good.

"I," said the donkey, shaggy and brown,
"I carried his mother up hill and down;
I carried her safely to Bethlehem town.
I," said the donkey, shaggy and brown.

"I," said the cow, all white and red,
"I gave him my manger for his bed;
I gave him my hay to pillow his head.
I," said the cow, all white and red.

"I," said the sheep with the curly horn,
"I gave him my wool for a blanket warm;
He wore my coat on Christmas morn.
I," said the sheep with the curly horn.

"I," said the dove from the rafters high,
"I cooed him to sleep so he would not cry;
I cooed him to sleep, my mate and I.
I," said the dove from the rafters high.

And every beast, by some good spell,
In the stable dark was glad to tell
Of the gift he gave Emmanuel,
The gift he gave Emmanuel.